May you discover
all of the
amazing things
that make you,
special,

Jh. Roms

THIS SWASH-BUCKLING BOOK BELONGS TO...

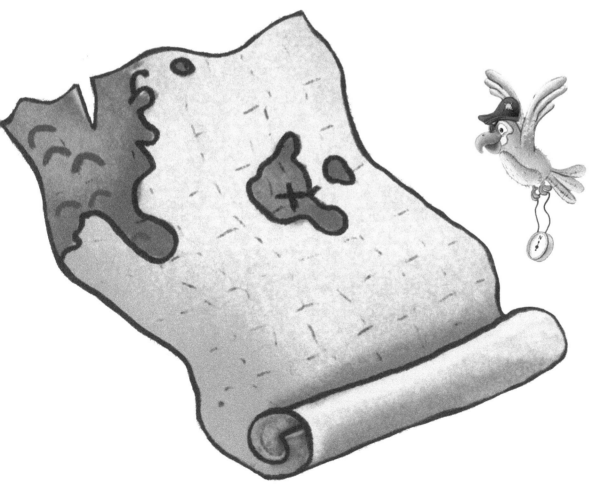

AUTH*OLOGIE
www.authologie.co.uk

Thank you to the team of editors who have helped to shape
'A Pirate at See'. Special mention to S. Robin Larin who provided
me with invaluable insights and support.

TO MY GREATEST TREASURES, FAITH AND DARIAN
AND ALL THE OTHER DARING KIDS WHO SEE THE
WORLD THROUGH ONE EYE.

– J.L. RAMES

J.L. RAMES

ADVENTURES WITH DARIAN

A Pirate at ~~Sea~~ SEE

Illustrated by
Daniel Wlodarski

Darian the Daring longed to be
the bravest, boldest, most daring
pirate who sailed the seven seas.

He dreamed of filling his treasure chest with glittering gold, silver, and jewels.

But all he had were...

rags,

seashells,

and broken spyglasses.

The Seven Seas Celebration was almost here. How could Darian compete in the Most Piratical Pirate Contest with nothing but a trunkful of junk?

Darian needed to track down some treasure - pronto.

But being a daring pirate wasn't easy...
Darian had a prosthetic eye, which left a
blind spot in his vision.

There were sword fights to dodge.

Fish guts to jump over.

Pesky parrots flying into his face.

Seeing the world with just one eye was tricky.

"Don't worry, Cap'n," said his first mate, Faith the Ferocious. "It only takes one eye to read a treasure map."

As Darian looked at the map
with his seeing eye, it was
a blotchy blur.

"I'm Daring Darian!" he said,
pretending to read the map.
"We'll sail the ocean swells,
follow the shining stars until..."

"We're here!" Darian announced.

Crunch!

"Cap'n! We've run aground!" cried Harold the Hideous.

"Not again," Darian groaned, his prosthetic eye almost popping out.

Darian needed to be careful or he might lose his prosthetic eye to Davy Jones's locker for good.

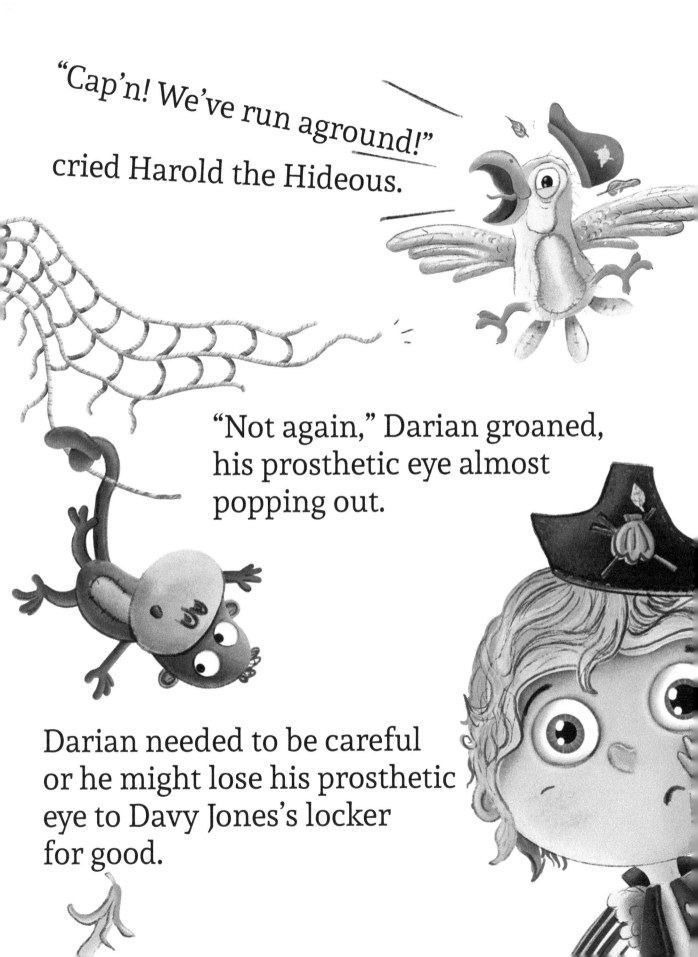

"Cap'n! Watch out!" yelled Faith.
Two slimy tentacles poked at his face.
"Kraken!" he yelped.

Darian rolled, reached into his loot, and flung a handful of seashells at the squid, which slithered out of sight.

"Shiver me timbers! That was close!" But the whole fiasco gave him an idea.

Rummaging in his loot, he got out a rag.
Carefully he tied it around his head,
attached a seashell, and covered his eye.

"Great idea, Cap'n!" said Victor the Vicious.

Darian's prosthetic eye was safe.
But more disasters came as he tried
to read the treasure maps.

They sailed east and
west, nearly swirling
down whirlpools.

They sailed north and
south, almost barging
into icebergs.

And when Darian reached for
his spyglass to search the sea...
...he stumbled and smacked
himself right in his seeing eye!

Ouch!

"How will I find treasure and win Most Piratical Pirate?" Darian stared at the spyglass in his hands. "I need to be able to read a treasure map!"
But then...

Darian gathered junk from his trunk and raced to his cabin.

He tinkered and toiled.

As the sun set, he returned to deck.

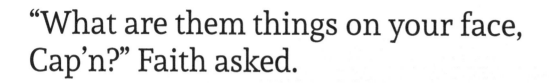

"What are them things on your face, Cap'n?" Faith asked.

"I call them eyeglasses. And now I can read maps!" The crew cheered. "There's no time for treasure hunting, we must get to the Seven Seas Celebration!" Darian couldn't disappoint his crew.

And they set sail!

As they pulled into port, Darian could see, in perfect focus, all the other pirates having a Jolly Roger time.

Swords slashed. Lobster claws clashed.

Yo-ho-hos echoed throughout the island.

All the other pirates' chests burst with gold, rubies, and shiny jewels.

Darian had his trunk of junk. His heart felt like an anchor dropping into the briny deep.

Suddenly, Odin the Oak towered over him.
The swashbuckling ceased.
The singing ended.
Even the pesky parrots stopped flying
into faces.

"What's that you're

wearing?" Odin yelled.

Darian gulped. "Eyeglasses, they help me see better."

"Eyeglasses?" roared Odin.

He drew in a huge breath.

Oh no! Was he about to laugh Darian out of the Seven Seas Celebration?

All around him, Darian heard pirates clamouring for his creations. Forgetting about treasure and competing, he got to work.

It turned out that many swashbucklers had eye troubles.

Jolly Joanie had damaged her eye in a fishing accident.

Frank the Fearless could only read a treasure map with one eye shut.

And Sassy Sally couldn't see anything far away.

Soon, most of the pirates had eye patches, or glasses, or even both.

Darian felt like the catch of the day as he was handed the award for Most Piratical Pirate!

Before long, requests and supplies arrived from all over the seven seas.

"What will you do with all this junk, Cap'n?" asked Faith.

Darian smiled as he looked at his chest full of letters, rags, seashells, and broken spyglasses.

It was the best treasure ever. "I'm going to be the bravest, boldest, most daring pirate of all: one who helps others."

AUTHOR'S NOTE

When my son Darian was only three years old, he was diagnosed with a rare eye condition called Coats' disease. Abnormal blood vessels in his eye leaked fluid, causing his retina to swell and begin to detach. His eye rapidly degenerated. Three months later, at SickKids in Toronto, we discovered that he had stage 5 Coats' disease and his retina had completely detached. The doctors had to remove his eye. Since then, our family has trekked forward with the same positive attitude Darian has, always willing to face any challenge with a smile.

Like Darian the Daring, my son Darian navigates the world with a prosthetic eye. The prosthetic eye is made of plastic acrylic and designed to match his real eye. Darian also wears protective eyeglasses with a polycarbonate lens to guard his seeing eye.

In this story, Darian invents both eye patches and eyeglasses to help himself and his friends who have low vision. While they weren't really invented by pirates, both patches and glasses are common vision management tools.

I hope this story inspires children with vision impairment to see themselves as heroes or as regular kids where vision impairment is not the focus of their life stories but merely a part of it. Let's create meaningful conversations where we celebrate our differences and respect the uniqueness in us all.

A SPECIAL NOTE

The Jack McGovern Coats' Disease Foundation – is a non-profit charitable foundation that was established in 2006 by the parents of Jack McGovern as a promise to their son that they would never rest until there was a cure for Coats' disease. The organization funds research to find a cure for Coats' disease and pediatric retinal disorders. The foundation seeks to raise awareness of Coats' disease to promote early and accurate diagnoses and is the preeminent resource for Coats' patients and their families.

coatsdiseasefoundation.org

Know the Glow – is a global non-profit leader in raising awareness of leukocoria (the Glow) and the childhood blinding diseases it can indicate. They work globally to eliminate preventable childhood blindness through early detection and treatment of these conditions. Know the Glow helps parents see their child's vision in a new light so that in the future no child goes blind from preventable eye diseases.

knowtheglow.org

CPSIA information can be obtained
at www.ICGtesting.com
Printed in the USA
LVHW050527140223
739390LV00008B/62